Naturally Me

This book is dedicated to any little boy or girl

who could use the occasional reminder that

they are just fine the way they naturally are.

When I wake up to start my day

I stretch my arms then smile and say

There's no one else I'd rather be

I'm proud to be naturally me

There's really nothing more unique

Than these six freckles on my cheek

Sometimes I count them one by one

And then start over when I'm done

My chocolate candy colored skin

The tiny dimple in my chin

This nose, these lips, this hair of mine

Belong to me and that's just fine

Sometimes I like to sing and hum

Dance to the beat of my own drum

And if I have to sing alone

Give me the biggest microphone

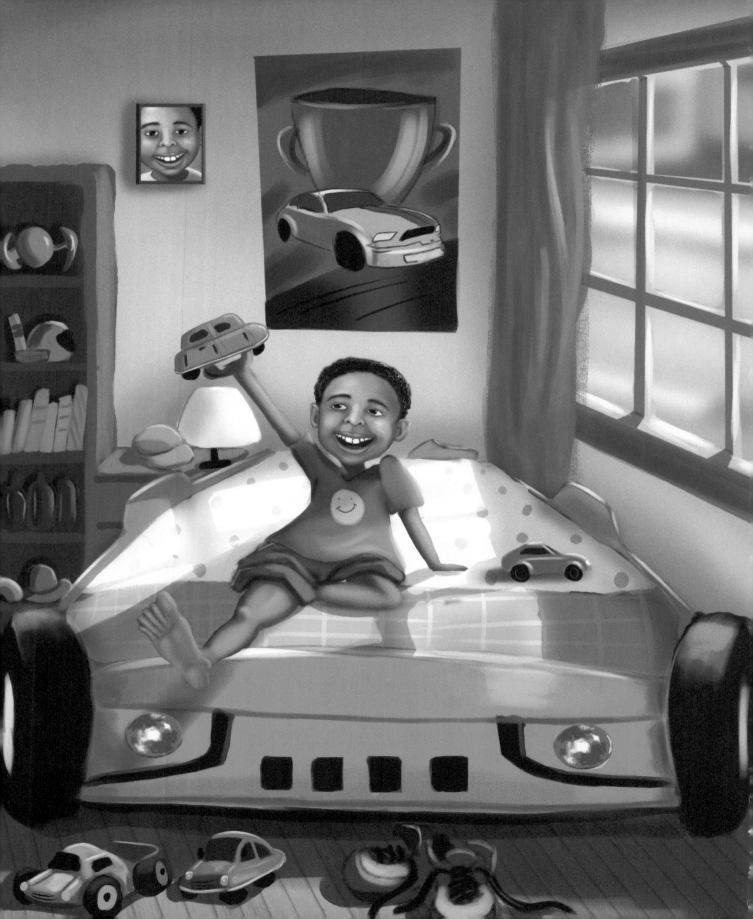

My golden honey colored skin

Long skinny toes, my toothy grin

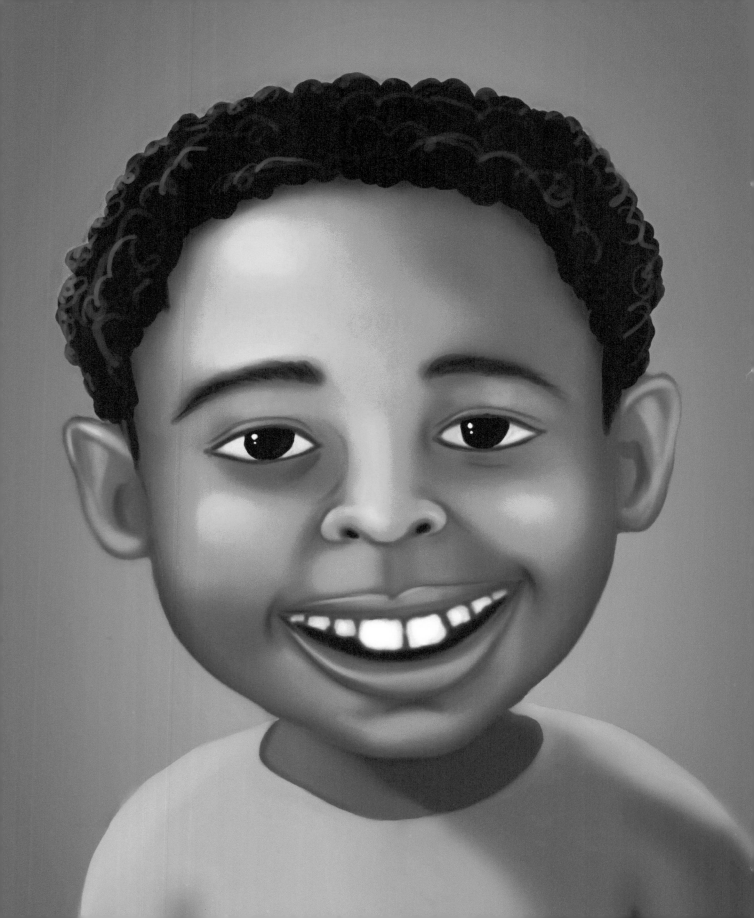

My teeth, these eyes, these toes of mine

Belong to me and that's just fine

If everybody looked the same

Then that would truly be a shame

How boring everything would be

If everybody looked like me

Some days my hair just seems so high

That it can almost touch the sky

I don't look like Jamie or Pam

I love myself the way I am

If a big genie said to me

That he could change my face for free

I'd tell him no, then grab my horn

And yell "I love how I was born"

At night before I end my day

I close my eyes then smile and say

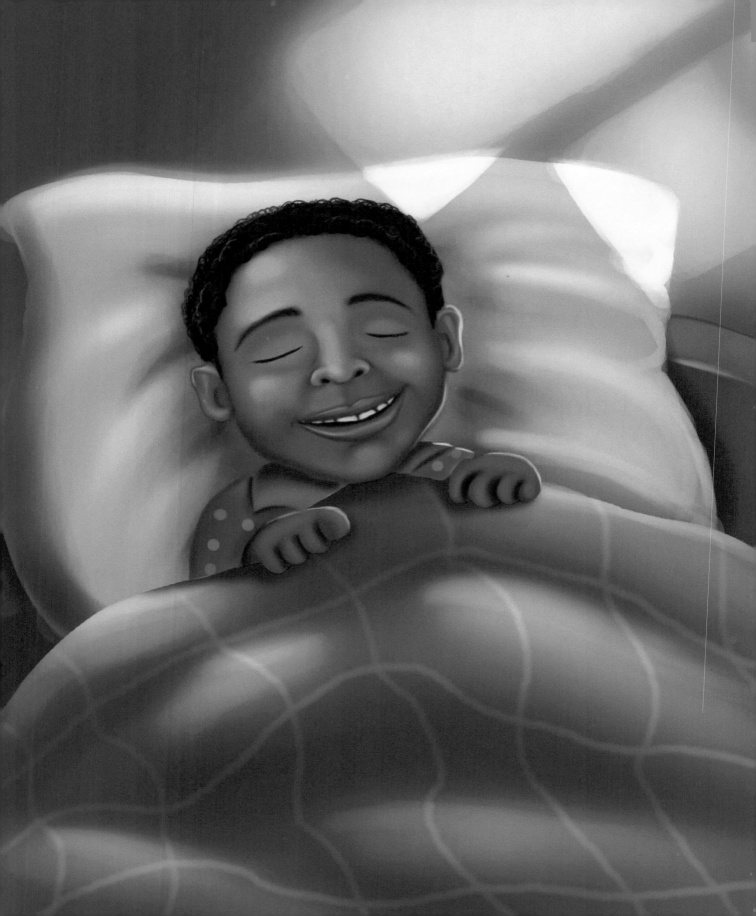

There's no one else I'd rather be

I'm proud to be naturally me

The End